Busy Baby

Annalena McAfee • Anthony Lewis

JM

Julia MacRae Books

LONDON SYDNEY AUCKLAND JOHANNESBURG

First published 1999

1 3 5 7 9 10 8 6 4 2

Text © 1999 Annalena McAfee
Illustrations © 1999 Anthony Lewis

Annalena McAfee and Anthony Lewis have asserted
their rights under the Copyright, Designs and Patents Act, 1988
to be identified as the author and illustrator of this work

First published in Great Britain 1999
by Julia MacRae
an imprint of Random House
20 Vauxhall Bridge Road, London, SW1V 2SA

Random House UK Limited Reg. No. 954009

A CIP catalogue record for this book is available from the British Library

ISBN 1 85681 544 7

Printed in Singapore

DAYS
OF THE WEEK

Monday

Tuesday

Wednesday

Thursday

Friday

Saturday

Sunday

MONDAY

No time to talk,
There's lots to do,
I must get going.
Can you come too?
Feed the birds,
Stroll in the park,
Swing on the swings,
Till it gets dark.

Cans and boxes
Piled up high.
Mustn't chat,
There's food to buy.
Watch me ride
The silver trolley.
Excuse me,
Can I have a lolly?

WEDNESDAY

Oh no, not again,

We did this last week

And I hated it then.

Splish, splash.

But now we've begun,

Playing with water

Can really be fun.

Can't stop, must rush,

Don't forget my special brush.

Should it be curls?

Or should it be straight?

I'm a busy baby

And can't be late.

FRIDAY

Stripes or ruffles?

Spots or lace?

Let's try the red one,

Just in case.

What about pink?

Or maybe blue?

I'm tempted by yellow.

How about you?

Look at the monkeys
Behind the bars.
They're looking back at me.
Do you think the keeper
Would mind very much
If I took them out to tea?

SUNDAY

Hurry, hurry,

Dust and mop,

Scrub and wipe,

No time to stop.

Sweep and polish,

Shake and shine,

Until the playroom's

Looking fine.

A little break for sleep and then

It's time to start the week again.

MONTHS
OF THE YEAR

 January

February

 March

April

 May

June

 July

August

 September

October

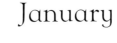 November

 December

January

Wrap up warm,
Hold on tight,
Watch out for
That snowball fight.
Climb the hill
To the very top,
Whizz on down
Until we drop.

Roll up! Roll up! The funfair's here.

The thrilling highlight of the year.

Does the big wheel appeal?

Would the water chute suit?

Do the coconuts make you shy?

Perhaps you're happier feet-on-the-ground,

Or maybe you'd rather fly?

Join the queue and very soon

You'll ride a rocket to the moon.

MARCH

Swooping and soaring above the hill,

Our paper bird just won't keep still.

Grip it firmly or else you'll find

You'll be leaving your family and friends behind.

APRIL

It makes me very happy,

But it makes the grown-ups frown:

Paddling in a puddle

As the rain pours down.

MAY

They like to skip and frolic
And they like a cuddle too,
And lambs all like their bottles
Just like me and you.

JUNE

Pull those weeds,
Sow those seeds,
Dig those holes,
Chase those moles.
Plant those flowers in a row,
Sun and showers will make them grow.

July

It's party time, as you can see.

Do come in and have some tea.

Perhaps you'd like a slice of cake?

It took all afternoon to bake.

We've games to play, I think you'll find.

A present? Why, how very kind!

AUGUST

With my bucket and spade,
I'll sit in the shade,
Make castles and daydream,
Till it's time for my ice-cream.

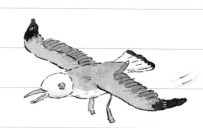

SEPTEMBER

Pears for the pastry,

Apples for the tart,

Currants for the flapjack,

When can we start?

Berries for the crumble,

Plums for the pie,

Damsons for the jelly,

By and by.

OCTOBER

Ghosts and ghouls
Don't frighten me.
I laugh at every curse,
But, may I ask,
Take off that mask?
Eek! That's even worse.

NOVEMBER

The bonfire's lit,

The sky flares up

With showers of sparkling rain.

Oooh! Aaah! Was that it?

Can we start again?

DECEMBER

We'll take the tree and dress it,
With globes of coloured light,
We'll wrap the many presents,
Sing carols through the night.
But when Santa comes a-calling,
We'll be dreaming in our beds.
For even busy babies need to
Rest their weary heads.